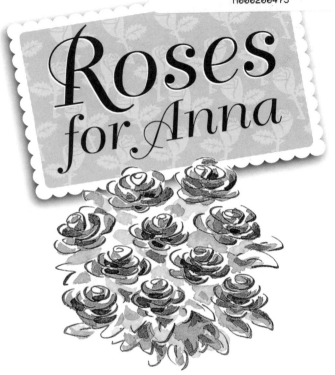

Roses for Anna

JAN WEEKS

Illustrated by Chantal Stewart

Rigby

Contents

CHAPTER ONE

Anna Forgets

Anna opened her eyes. She sat up in bed and stretched her arms into the air. It was Saturday, and Saturday was her very favorite day.

On Saturday mornings, she didn't have to jump out of bed to get ready to go to school. Anna liked school. But she liked staying at home, too.

Anna scratched her head. She had a feeling that today was a special Saturday, but she couldn't remember why. Nothing special had been planned. They weren't going anywhere. They weren't expecting any visitors.

"Oh, no!" she cried, suddenly remembering. It was the sixth of May. It was her mother's birthday and she'd forgotten all about it.

It was no good looking in her piggy bank on the shelf. It was empty. She'd spent all her money on a book about horses. It was too late to make anything for her mother. What was she going to do?

Daddy would have given her money, but Daddy didn't live with them anymore. He'd moved away to another town.

"I'll just have to solve the problem by myself," she thought as she hopped out of bed. "But how?"

Mom and Anna's brother Tom were sitting in the kitchen eating their breakfast.

"Hello, Anna," her mother said as Anna sat at the table. "Did you sleep well?"

Anna nodded. She hoped her brother wouldn't mention their mother's birthday. She didn't want her mother to know she had forgotten. Not when Anna's mother always remembered *their* birthdays.

It was then that she saw the big box of chocolates on the table.

"I bought these for Mom for her birthday," Tom said, looking pleased with himself.

"They cost a lot. What are you giving her, Anna?"

"It's a surprise," she answered. "Happy birthday, Mom. I'll give you your surprise later."

"No matter what it is," her mother said, smiling at Anna, "I'm sure it will be wonderful."

"I hope so," Anna mumbled, but not loudly enough for anyone to hear.

CHAPTER TWO

Mrs. Duffy's Prize Roses

After breakfast, Anna went outside. She could see her next-door neighbor working in her front garden. Mrs. Duffy loved gardening. People said she grew the best flowers in town. They especially liked her roses.

Anna stood on her front lawn and looked at Mrs. Duffy's prize roses. Anna's mother loved roses.

She especially liked the long-stemmed red roses that Mrs. Duffy grew by her side fence.

Anna thought about Mrs. Duffy's long-stemmed red roses. A bunch of long-stemmed red roses would make a wonderful present for her mother's birthday.

Mrs. Duffy paid a lot of money for her rose bushes. She entered them in flower shows and almost always won first prize. Whenever Anna went into her house, she saw all the blue ribbons that Mrs. Duffy had won. She kept them on display near her front door.

Anna knew Mrs. Duffy would not want to give away any of her prize roses. And it wouldn't be right to steal the roses. Anna's mother would not want a present that had been stolen.

At last, Anna had an idea. She decided to go next door to talk to Mrs. Duffy.

CHAPTER THREE

One Thing Leads to Another

Mrs. Duffy was busy pulling out weeds. There was a big pile of them on the grass beside her. She looked up when she saw Anna coming toward her.

"Mrs. Duffy," Anna said, coming straight to the point, "it's my mother's birthday today. If I did some work for you, would you let me have a bunch of your long-stemmed red roses? I know my mother would like them."

Mrs. Duffy thought for a minute. "There is something you can do for me, Anna," she said. "I need my cutting shears to cut the roses, but I loaned them to Mr. Sams. Would you go across the street to ask Mr. Sams if I could have my cutting shears? Then I can cut my roses and give you some."

"Sure!" Anna answered, pleased that the job Mrs. Duffy had given her would not take her very long to do.

She ran across the street to where Mr. Sams lived. He was busy painting his house. There was white paint all over his shirt.

"Good morning, Anna," he said, stopping to smile at her. "What can I do for you?"

"Mr. Sams," Anna asked, "could Mrs. Duffy please have her cutting shears back? She would like to cut some roses, but she needs her cutting shears."

Mr. Sams nodded. "Of course she can. It was very nice of her to lend them to me. But first, could I ask you to do something for me? The cutting shears are on the top shelf in my shed, and I need a ladder to reach them and to finish my painting. Could you please ask Dr. Perez if I can borrow her ladder? My ladder has a broken rung."

"No problem," Anna answered, nodding.

Dr. Perez was Mr. Sams' neighbor. Anna found her near the side of her house, washing her new car. "Good morning, Anna," she said.

"Dr. Perez," Anna said, "could Mr. Sams please borrow your ladder? His ladder has a broken rung and he needs a ladder to get some cutting shears and to finish painting his house."

"Certainly," Dr. Perez said. "But I can't get it right now. I'm washing my car, but I could finish it more quickly if I had a hose. My hose has a big hole in it. Would you ask Mr. Lin if I could borrow his hose? Then I can quickly finish washing my car and help you."

"I'll go and ask him," Anna answered.

CHAPTER FOUR

More and More Neighbors

Anna walked along the street to where Mr. Lin lived. Mr. Lin was in his backyard, hanging out the laundry.

"Could Dr. Perez borrow your hose, please?" Anna asked. "Her hose has a hole in it, and she needs one to finish washing her new car."

Mr. Lin nodded. "Of course," he said. "But first, would you ask Mr. Small if I could borrow some of his clothespins. I'm not going to have enough clothespins to hang out all this laundry, and I want to get everything dry while the sun's shining."

Anna sighed and ran to Mr. Small's house. He was on his front porch, in the middle of giving his dog a bath. He smiled when he saw Anna.

"Mr. Small," Anna said, as she bent to pet the very wet dog, "Mr. Lin has sent me to ask if he could borrow some clothespins. He doesn't have enough to hang out all his laundry, and he wants to get everything dry while the sun is still shining."

"He can borrow as many clothespins as he likes," Mr. Small said. "But first, would you mind doing something for me? Ask Miss Bell if she'd let me borrow some soap. I used up all my soap washing my dog, and I need some more. Once I've finished washing and drying my dog, I can help you."

Anna walked across the street. Her legs were beginning to feel tired. She wondered what Miss Bell would ask her to do.

Miss Bell was in her kitchen. She'd just finished baking a big chocolate cake. It smelled delicious.

"Miss Bell," Anna asked, "would you mind if Mr. Small borrowed some soap? He used up all his soap giving his dog a bath and he needs some more. Then he can finish washing and drying his dog and help me."

"Of course he can," Miss Bell answered. "But first, would you mind doing something for me?"

Anna waited to hear what it would be. Was Miss Bell about to send her on another errand?

Anna was beginning to feel like she was running around in circles.

"Have some cake. You look quite worn out, my dear."

"Thank you," Anna answered. "I would love some cake."

CHAPTER FIVE

Happy Birthday, Mom!

After Anna had finished her cake, Miss Bell gave her some soap to give to Mr. Small.

Mr. Small thanked Anna for the soap and gave her some clothespins to give to Mr. Lin.

Mr. Lin took the clothespins and gave Anna his hose.

Anna took the hose to Dr. Perez, who gave Anna her ladder.

Dr. Perez helped Anna carry the ladder to Mr. Sams, who put Mrs. Duffy's cutting shears in a bag and gave them to Anna.

Mrs. Duffy thanked Anna for the cutting shears and gave Anna 10 of her best long-stemmed red roses.

"Happy birthday, Mom!" said Anna, as she gave the beautiful roses to her mother. "I told you I was going to give you a surprise."

Anna's mother was delighted with her red roses. She said Anna couldn't have given her a better present.

But Anna's mother didn't have a vase. She turned to Anna. "Anna," she said, "would you mind running next door to see if we could borrow a vase from Mr. Parkes?"

"Oh, no," thought Anna. "Here we go again . . ."